100%

MATCH

Patrick C. Harrison III

This is a work of fiction. None of the people, places, or events described in this novel actually exist or happened. Not that I'm aware of…

PC3 HORROR

Full Contact Fiction

pc3horror.com
Instagram@thepc3
Etsy.com/shop/pc3books
Slasher@PC3
pc3horror.substack.com
pc3@pc3horror.com

DEDICATION

For all the fellas out there in search of *THE ONE*

CONTENTS

ACKNOWLEDGMENTS

This depraved tale was originally supposed to be in an anthology published by Macabre Ladies. For reasons I'm not privy to, that book was permanently delayed. But without the prompting of Eleanor Merry, this story would not exist. So, thank you, Eleanor.

A Day in the Life

0.001752% of relationships end in homicide.

As a fast-food worker, I'm already at a disadvantage finding a life partner. The number one—*numero uno!*—least desired profession women want for their mate, is a fast-food worker. Being a fry cook and burger flipper, like myself, is probably the worst among fast food workers, but I've been unable to find studies stating this.

I'm working on upgrading my desirability, though. Statistically speaking, elementary educators enjoy the most success in long term relationships. That incident at the state park in Arkansas is causing some minor delays in me being accepted into a teaching program, however. But that was a complete misunderstanding, I assure you.

My alarm goes off at 8am, like usual, but, like usual, I've been lying here awake for the last hour or so, thinking about that perfect lady—my match—and rubbing gently on my morning wood. I don't bring myself to climax, though. It's a common misconception that men are more adept at connecting with the opposite sex after their spunk has been blasted from their ball-sacks. In reality, they're less likely to make the oft required first move, such as striking up a conversation with an unfamiliar potential partner. Thus, orgasms are relegated to just before bedtime, when the chances of connecting with a potential mate are virtually impossible.

I turn off the alarm and get up and walk into the bathroom and take a leak. It takes a while for my hardness to dissipate and for the pee to flow, but eventually success is achieved. I can't see my wienie, my little pecker, my loving love rod, unless I lean forward. My belly blocks it from view. It's also not a particularly large specimen.

69% of women prefer the "dad bod" as opposed to a chiseled physique. This is encouraging, but my living carcass is a little heftier than the typical dad bod. On average, women prefer an erect penis size of 6.3 inches, slightly above normal. I fall far short of this, unfortunately.

After performing my function at the toilet, I flush it away and tuck my business back into my boxer briefs (it's well-documented that most women prefer boxer briefs over any other male undergarment) and move over to the counter where I grab my toothbrush and squeeze on whitening toothpaste and begin brushing. I look at myself in the mirror as I do this, seeing the gleam of fluorescent light on my bald head and the day's-worth of stubble on my double chin.

43% of women thirty-five to forty-five find bald men attractive. That would be somewhat promising if I weren't thirty. 83% of women prefer a mate older than themselves. Among women younger than myself, only 19% find baldness attractive.

After brushing my teeth, I gargle some mouthwash and spit it down the drain, then I shave. While 60% of women in the southern United States (where I live) prefer men with facial hair, my facial hair grows in odd patches rather than the lush fullness favored by ladies. After shaving, I apply lotion to my face and body, then rub a fair amount of anti-perspirant under my arms. Though a surprising amount of women find the scent of a sweaty man enticing, the percentage that like perspiration stains in the armpits of a man's clothing is so miniscule that it's almost beyond calculation.

My nose is clogged. Happens all the time in spring. I tear off some toilet paper and blow my nose. The result is a yellowish-green glob of snot.

Folding the toilet paper over, I blow again and expel a little more, though not as globby and not as yellowish-green. I retrieve a zip-lock baggy from a drawer and place the snotty tissue inside it and seal it up and place it next to my wallet and house keys in the bedroom.

Next, I get dressed in the required work clothes—black shoes, black slacks, and a light-blue t-shirt that has a Jim's Burger Joint logo on the left breast and proclaims *Mangle County's Best Burger!* on the back. After donning my clothes, I go to the kitchen and make and consume a breakfast consisting of one sliced tomato, two boiled eggs, a bowl of oatmeal with blueberries, and a glass of apple juice. This combination of foods is supposed to provide me with sufficient energy and mental acuity to start my day, keeping me sharp in case engaging in conversation with a woman is required. Coffee is also a suitable addition to breakfast, though I've determined the tendency for this beverage to cause bad breath and stained teeth renders it less necessary. I do drink it on occasion though.

Women prefer men that are knowledgeable in a variety of things, especially perceived masculine things. So, after eating breakfast and washing the dishes, I use my phone to watch a video on how to change a fuel pump and then one on how to make a picnic table. I read a few articles from various news websites, followed by the latest from *Cosmopolitan*, a story detailing the most comfortable brands of thong underwear for women who work on their feet.

Of course, I have to don my glasses to read all this. Women are largely torn on the attractiveness of men with glasses. On one hand, they view men with glasses as goal-oriented and intelligent. On the other, they see glasses as a sign of genetic inferiority. Especially if the glasses required are quite thick, like my own. I did, however, acquire stylish thick-rimmed glasses that suggest a quirkiness that most ladies find alluring.

It's time to go to work. I put my wallet, keys,

and the zip-lock bag containing the snotty tissue into my pockets. I add an empty zip-lock bag to my pocket too. I grab my lunch pail from the fridge (women prefer men with lunch pails over men with brown paper sacks; the paper sacks are suggestive of childishness) and head out the door, locking up as I go.

I live in a nice neighborhood. Though it's an older part of town, the fact that I own my own house is extremely positive. In the eyes of a woman, home ownership suggests I am mature, hard-working, and financially stable. Women also consider men that own a home twice as datable. The only reason I own my own home is because my morbidly obese mother drank a little too much home-brewed cyanide tea on a hot summer day, leaving her only son with the house. But the ladies don't need to know that.

I don't have a car, however. Well, I do—Mother's old 1999 Buick—but I'm not allowed to drive it. My license was suspended after an unfortunate incident involving a raccoon, a bottle of castor oil, and a road trip down to Galveston.

96% of women want their partner to have a vehicle. A devastating stat. Honestly, I'm surprised it's not higher.

Luckily, Jim's Burger Joint is within walking distance. It's 1.6 miles from my house, meaning I walk 3.2 miles per day, counting only the commute. I probably walk four or more miles if I take into account the rest of my day. This should be beneficial to my physique and overall health, though I've yet to notice any real changes to my frame.

63% of women want a man who exercises regularly. Though, this is misleading. They don't generally want men who spend hours a day at the gym. They want men that are strong, but not overly muscular. They want men that are fit, but not fat free. That being said, my walks back and forth from work are probably not sufficient. So, during the fifteen-minute breaks at work, I do standing hip thrusts to work my glutes and core.

To work my upper body, I sometimes throw punches—shadow boxing, I think it's called. I also throw things when the opportunity arises; like if a cat walks into my yard, I'll throw it into the street.

The late morning sun feels good on my face. It's still early enough in the year for the heat not to be exhausting. Walks to work in the summer months are grueling. I have a decent tan from these walks. Regarding white males, like myself, women prefer a medium tan over dark tans or none at all. I guess I have what could be called a medium tan, though that's very nonspecific.

I'm about halfway to work when I see Miss Danbury walking from her house to check the mail. It's too early for the mail to have arrived, which she should know since she's lived in the neighborhood for over half a century. But when you're eighty, I suppose an extra walk or two to the mailbox is good for the old body. Unless she were to fall and break a hip or something. She carries a cane and walks very slow. Painfully

9

slow.

"Good morning, Bartholomew," Miss Danbury says as I walk by.

Yes, my name is Bartholomew. Studies have shown women prefer men with short names, like John, Jack, Curt, and so on. I tell people to call me Bart but, as you probably suspect, I then get compared to a popular cartoon character. My last name is Bartley. I have no middle name. So, I have to introduce myself to new acquaintances as Bart Bartley. It's quite comical, I know.

I tell Miss Danbury hello and give her a wave and move on. She was probably a decent catch in her younger years. Seems nice enough and her sagging face shows hints of attractiveness, marred by time. She's a widow, but I have no intention of making a move on her. For one thing, the age difference. For another, studies of widows have shown that they *always* hold their deceased spouse in equal or even *higher* regard than the mate they replace them with.

I *have* masturbated to Miss Danbury three

10

times, though. Once while I was at work.

I leave the neighborhood and cross an intersection and am passing by a Chevron station when a cricket goes hopping across the sidewalk in front of me. Lunging forward, I stomp on the cricket, feeling it crunch beneath my shoe. Turning my shoe to the side, I notice half the bug sticks to the rubber tread, while the rest of it remains on the sidewalk. It's gooey looking. I scrape the cricket remains off my shoe with the end of my fingernail, then pick up both crushed halves, at the same time removing the empty zip-lock baggy from my pocket. As I put the cricket into the baggy, I notice a kid on a bicycle in the gas station parking lot is watching me and chewing gum. I smile politely and seal the bag and continue to work.

I get to work right on time and clock in. I'm always on time, if not early. 69% of women prefer a man who is punctual, or at least able to keep a schedule. After putting my lunch pail in the breakroom fridge and donning an apron, I go to my work station and turn on the grill and fryers. The grill sizzles and smokes from the remnants of old burgers. The canola oil in the fryers smells somewhat sour and I really should change it out, but I figure it's got another day or two before it would be noticeable to customers.

We open at 10:30. Too early for lunch, in my opinion, but I don't own the place. Jim Clark does. He's a pompous fellow, loud-mouthed and vulgar, with a red face, yellow teeth, and bad breath. He wears a tie to work at his burger joint for some reason, and on more than one occasion he's leaned over my fryers to inspect whatever owners inspect and seared off the end of his tie. Jim once had a week-long stomach condition that landed him in the hospital after eating a triple cheeseburger I cooked for him. Actually, I was surprised he survived.

"Bart, where is Hector?" Jim says, staring at me in the kitchen from his spot at the front register.

I have no idea why he thinks I should know

where Hector is. Hector is always late. I shrug and scrape at the grill with the end of my spatula. The black crud that comes off looks like it could've come from the inside of a septic tank.

Jim groans and says something I don't understand. Something about "no good piece of" something or other. I'm not sure if he's referring to me or Hector. Not that it matters. One January, Jim slipped and fell going out the back door of the burger joint after someone poured dishwater over the concrete steps back there.

Five minutes later, Hector walks in. Jim yells at him for being late and tells him one more time and he's gone.

Hector says, "Yo, I'm here, dog. And we ain't even got any customers."

"It doesn't matter!" Jim says, a little too forcefully. "You should be here when the schedule says you should be here!"

"You need to chill, dog."

This is a scene that plays out almost every

13

day. Jim always tells Hector he'll be fired next time, and Hector always calls Jim a dog.

"Sup, Shorty," Hector says, giving me the 'sup nod.

I'm not really short. I'm five-eight, shorter than the average male, but not *short*. As you likely know, most women prefer men on the tall side. However, shorter women are typically more inclined to date men who are also of smaller than average stature. So, I don't really consider my height a hindrance in my quest for love.

Hector calls me Shorty because he's six-five. Absurdly tall, in my opinion. Hector, a Latino, has slicked back black hair, fake diamond earrings, too many tattoos to count, and baggy clothes that I think look ridiculous. He also smells of marijuana all the time. If his stories are to be believed, he is a real success with the ladies. Though, we measure success differently. All those things about his appearance are clear indicators, studies show, of a man who is not

14

seeking a life partner.

If they have tattoos, they screw. This is true of men and women alike. If they smoke, they poke. Also true, studies show.

I'm not simply looking to get my man rod wet. I can just as easily derive sexual pleasure from mayonnaise jars or crawdad holes. And have. No, I'm looking for my true love, my life partner, my 100% perfect match. So, when it comes to women, I stay away from tattoos and smoke. When it comes to Hector, I'm unimpressed by his exploits.

I nod to Hector and tell him good morning and wave my spatula at him. Some of the black gunk falls off and sizzles on the grill.

"Yo, Shorty, you should have seen this banging chick I was with last night."

I smile at Hector without comment. Luckily, the drive-thru bell sounds, indicating we have a customer. Hector works the drive-thru until noon, at which time Lacy arrives and Hector goes between helping me package meals and helping

Jim take orders from the dining area. Hector takes the order—a double cheeseburger with all the fixings and a large fry.

I take two frozen meat patties from the cooler and toss them on the grill. Then I throw an order of fries in the fryer. I take the squashed cricket from my pocket and throw it in the fryer with the fries. While this cooks, I retrieve buns, cheddar cheese, lettuce, tomato, onions, and pickles from the bar at my work station. The customer ordered the burger with mayonnaise, so I get one of the large mayonnaise jars. I don't think it's one I've masturbated into before. But it's hard to keep track.

When the patties are done cooking, I put the burger together. In between the patties I apply the yellowish-green snot from the zip-locked tissue in my pocket. I spread it out over the cheese, the heat of the patties making it more liquefied and less globby, making it look like a secret sauce of some kind. With the food prepared, I wrap the burger in paper and dump the fries into a cardboard container. Hector takes it from there.

The day goes by about like any other. It gets busy around lunch. I make lots of burgers and cook lots of fries. I blow my nose in a piece of lettuce once and find a roach under the fryers, which I add to an old man's milkshake. I do my standing hip thrusts in the breakroom on break and Jim comes in asking what the hell I'm doing. Lacy comes in at noon looking slutty as ever, smelling of cigarettes and dirty diapers. She has a newborn and doesn't know who the father is. Not me, that's for sure. Lacy is about as far away from my match as a woman could be. She's had more penis in her than...I don't know...a penis factory. A lot is what I mean. Not my type. Nevertheless, she's a nice enough person and I've even masturbated to her thirty-two times, once in the dumpster behind Jim's and another time at the DMV. Anyway, my shift ends at 6pm and I clock-out on the dot and walk home and throw a cat out of my yard and watch a documentary on how the amputation of a limb affects long-term relationships.

After the show, I take a poop into a zip-lock and put it in the fridge next to a used jar of mayonnaise and Mimi, the next-door neighbor's dead Chihuahua. She'll need to be used soon, before she spoils. I take a shower and wash myself with sandalwood-scented soap—voted the best smelling among women twenty-five to thirty-five—then brush my teeth and wash my mouth again.

Before heading to bed, I shoot the kid I have chained up in the basement. 76% of women can be convinced that the sound of a gunshot was actually a car backfiring.

Debra

I went on a date with a blonde once. Statistically speaking, blondes are the least likely to give you a lasting relationship. You'd think it was redheads, but you'd be wrong. In fact, non-blondes who dye their hair blonde instantly become more likely to cheat and otherwise see themselves out of whatever current relationship they're in. I've read the data. All the same, I went on a date with a blonde.

Her name was Debra and she worked at a department store and had aspirations of becoming a doctor. She would never be a doctor;

I knew this right off. Sometimes you can just tell by the way people talk that they're not as smart as they think. Debra would say stuff like 'intensive purposes' instead of 'intents and purposes.' And 'pacific' instead of 'specific.' Stuff someone smart enough to get through medical school would know, in my opinion.

Still, this didn't mean she would make a bad mate. It didn't mean we couldn't form a lasting bond.

Though I don't put much stock in horoscopes, Debra was a Gemini and I'm an Aquarius; they're supposed to go good together. But I didn't hinge my hopes on astrological superstitions. Debra wore minimal makeup, didn't go to a tanning salon, had only one social media account, and, while she exercised, she did not do so daily. All of these traits are indicative of a person able to maintain a long-term relationship. She also didn't drink, smoke, or have tattoos. And she wasn't a vegan.

100% of vegans are snooty and attention-seeking, and they're impossible to please.

Debra was blonde, like I said, with brown eyes and medium-sized breasts and a bit of a frumpy midsection and droopy bottom. With the exception of her hair, her other physical attributes were such that she wouldn't be a sufferer of daily romantic advances from other suitors. Given my own physical downfalls, this was obviously preferable.

We had dinner at Applebee's. Being the gentleman that I am, I gave Debra the opportunity to choose where we went, but she declined. (If a woman ever freely decides where to eat, alarm bells should immediately go off.) So, I decided on Applebee's, a place that isn't overly expensive, which would falsely give the impression that I was either desperate or financially loaded, but also not too cheap, like Jim's Burger Joint, which would give the impression that my romantic interest was insufficient.

Conversation went well in the beginning. I

talked about wanting to be a teacher and Debra talked about wanting to be a doctor. I talked about a birdhouse I built for my backyard, without divulging that I fastened a mousetrap on the inside and rigged it weekly. She talked about the television shows she enjoyed, none of which were reality TV.

65% of people—no matter their gender, race, or sexual orientation—who watch reality TV have a diminished sense of self-worth and have virtually no hope for humankind as a whole.

So, things were going fine. Then Debra asked me to tell her one secret about myself, something no one else knew. This should have sent up alarm bells. But so pleased with the evening was I, that I considered the question happily and answered honestly. I told her about the time I visited a random person at the nursing home, taking with me a bag containing a bearded dragon, a cucumber, and a mallet.

Debra was not impressed by my escapades at the nursing home. The night ended poorly.

Two days later, Debra would die after spraying herself with hydrofluoric acid that had somehow made its way into her perfume bottle. Sad. But she wasn't going to be a doctor anyway.

Missed Opportunity

56% of women desire a man who is innovative, self-motivated, and willing to take risks.

Hector is late again but only by two minutes and Jim Clark's rants are somewhat abated. The first order of the day is for six burgers—hold the cheese—and no fries. I use the Mimi meat to make these burgers. Chihuahuas make a surprising amount of meat for their size. I season them the same way as the regular patties and they smell pretty similar cooking. Jim later eats one for lunch.

Lacy spends most of the day complaining that her baby—who she named Xander—won't stop crying and that she has a date tonight but is having trouble finding a babysitter and that her mom, Xander's grandmother, is unwilling to watch Xander because her ex-boyfriend is being released from prison today and they're going to the casino in Oklahoma to celebrate.

When I leave the burger joint that evening, I walk across the street to the grocery store to get a few things I need—milk, canned tuna, one corn on the cob, and mayonnaise. I hate having to carry milk all the way back home but I do it once a week. It's good exercise, I suppose. I grab a basket and go to the fruits and vegetables section.

Studies have shown that women who spend five or more minutes in the fruits and vegetables section at the grocery store are 54% more likely to have—or *want* to have—a family, compared to those who spend less than five minutes in the same section. Presently, there are two women in the fruits and vegetables section, a young Latina woman who could be around twenty-five and an elderly Asian woman.

93% of Asian American women are married before they hit forty. 81% of that 93% remain married their entire lives. Thus, even though 14% of women will wear a wedding band for the sole purpose of warding off romantic advances, I take the wedding band on the Asian lady's finger to be genuine.

She's too old anyway and appears to have arthritis, which can hinder a woman's ability to jerk off her male counterpart.

The Latina woman is wearing incredibly tight clothing and her breasts are the size of the cantaloupes she's looking at. Her nipples are visible through the white shirt she wears. While she will make satisfactory masturbatory material this evening, she is obviously not suitable as a lifelong mate.

69% of women who wear blouses exposing their nipples in public are more interested in

short-term   physical   relationships   than
sustainable romance.

I grab my corn on the cob and move on.

"Bartholomew Bartley, is that you?" I hear
someone say as I'm turning onto the canned
goods aisle.

Spinning, I see that it's Mr. Higgins, my old
middle school principal. I tell him it is indeed me.

"Goodness, it's been years, Bartholomew,"
he says, smiling incredibly wide. His hair has
greyed since I last saw him.

I agree it's been years.

"I heard about your mother passing a few
years back. That's so very tragic."

I agree it's very tragic.

"So, what are you up to? How has life since
middle school treated you?"

I tell him life is fine and that I work at Jim's,
but that that's only temporary because I'm
planning on becoming a teacher.

"A teacher? My goodness, that would be
wonderful! We need lots of good teachers in

Mangle County, you know."

I agree we do. After an awkward moment, we bid each other goodbye and say it was nice seeing each other and such as that. He fails to mention what he caught me doing in the janitor's closet when I was in the 8th grade and I'm glad for this.

After gathering my groceries, I go to the register where a young lady—probably only sixteen or seventeen—begins scanning my items. Her nametag identifies her as Swelly, an odd name, and she has a bunch of jewelry in her face and wears black lipstick. There was a time in my life when I would have found this stuff rather attractive, but that was about fifteen long gone years ago. Swelly asks if I want my milk in a bag and I tell her no thanks.

32% of women with multiple facial piercings are involved in regular drug use. 16% of people—any gender—who wear black lipstick on a daily basis have frequent thoughts of suicide.

The sky is already a dark blue as I walk out

into the parking lot, with a dozen or so stars twinkling and only a sliver of the sun still peaking over the horizon. I head toward the street, intending to cross it and take a right toward my house, when I see a woman's wallet fall from her purse as she gets out of her car. She appears not to notice and closes her door and walks toward the grocery store with her walletless purse slung over her shoulder.

Shuffling over to her car, I set the milk on the pavement and scoop up her wallet and hold it over my head, hollering "ma'am" to get her attention. She turns around, looking startled, looking frightened, looking like someone who thinks they're about to get robbed.

"Yes?" she says, her light-brown eyes wide.

I tell her she dropped her wallet.

"Oh, goodness," she says and walks timidly to where I stand. "That's very kind of you. A lot of people in this world would have taken it. Thank you."

I tell her to think nothing of it. She has wavy

29

brown hair to her shoulders, styled nice but not eccentric. She's heavyset but not fat. Her breasts are full but she's conservatively dressed, so as not to draw attention to her curves. She wears little if any makeup, yet her face is pleasing in a simple way. She takes the wallet from my outstretched hand.

"Thank you, again," she says, smiling. "You're truly kind."

I nod, wanting to say something more but completely unable to find the words.

"Goodbye," she says, nodding back and turning and walking to the grocery store, the whole time with me standing there like an idiot deaf-mute.

When she's disappeared inside the store, I go back to walking home, almost forgetting to pick up the milk. The walk home is a blur. I've done this a dozen or more times, where I unexpectedly come across a promising candidate for a life partner and end up blowing it by either not saying anything or, worse, saying something incredibly dumb.

One time, I was attending the county fair, checking out the concessions and different vendors. There was this lady who had a table selling handmade jewelry. She definitely looked like a potential mate, so I approached her table and fondled the earrings and necklaces she had on display. She asked how my day was going. My garbled response was to inform her that it was Fat Tuesday. I wasn't lying. It *was* Fat Tuesday. But, seeing as she was a rather hefty woman, she understandably took offense. She quickly noted that I wasn't so slim myself and called me an asshole and advised I shop elsewhere.

98.3% of women do not like being called fat.

When I reach the house, I notice the same cat from the previous evening camped out in my front yard. I put the gallon of milk in the crook of my arm carrying the other groceries and stoop down and snatch up the cat before it can run away. Instead of throwing it, I bring it inside with me. It's kind of a multi-colored cat. Not altogether ugly. I let it roam around while I put away the milk and mayonnaise.

I go take a leak and pick a few nose hairs, which I store away in zip-lock bags, and come back out and kick the cat in the face and then make myself a tuna sandwich. The cat is very interested in the tuna sandwich despite the kick in the face. I let her or him—not sure which—take a bite. She or he seems to enjoy it.

I put a bowl of milk out for the cat then watch a documentary on heroin addiction among transvestites in Wisconsin then cut up the dead kid in my basement and vacuum seal the pieces and store them in the freezer down there. After all that, I go to take a shower, taking the cat and the corn on the cob with me.

Wendy

22% of modern relationships begin online.

The internet seems like it would be the perfect place to meet your special someone, especially if you want a specific type of special someone. Maybe you live in a moderately small town, like myself, and can't seem to find that special someone in your community. The internet should be the perfect way for you to connect with those outside your community. The problem with internet dating is that so many people lie about themselves.

A staggering 89% of women have used

filters when posting pictures of themselves online. Equally staggering, 58% of the populous admits to fibbing, lying, or exaggerating when filling out their profiles on dating apps and websites.

I met a woman on such a website. Her name was Wendy. Wendy DarkPoet was the handle she used on this dating site. (I didn't know it then, but 97% of people who fancy themselves dark poets are talentless fools who type out gibberish and post it online and call it art.) She had dark hair and dark eyes and wore dark clothing. All this was fine with me. She also claimed to be a recluse who didn't like being around people. Excellent; true love is only really experienced when you're alone together. She said she'd never been in love and dreamed of the day when she'd be united with her soul mate. Because the world, she explained, created a perfect match for everyone.

All this was music to my ears. I agreed with nearly everything she said. We began talking regularly through the website messenger. Pretty soon, we exchanged phone numbers and were texting nonstop. I suggested phone calls, but Wendy always declined, saying that she felt embarrassed talking on the phone and she was afraid she wouldn't know what to say. I consented. It's understandable for someone who is a recluse, someone who isn't overly sociable, to not want to talk on the phone. This is what I told myself, my brain foggy with desire for her.

This went on for months.

I was spending a significant portion of my time reading her poetry and trying to make sense of it. She had this one poem about a vampire and a witch making love, and it used the F-word nineteen times. The poem was barely a page long. Whatever emotional response her poetry was supposed to trigger, it was having little effect on me, unless you count confusion and revulsion. I figured it was just over my head.

Eventually, I convinced her to meet up. She

lived about four hours away. We met at a seafood restaurant in Shreveport, Louisiana that was about an hour from her home and three from mine. This was before my license was suspended, so I'm meaning three hours of driving time, not walking time. The distance bothered me a bit, yes. But, surprisingly, 60% of long-distance relationships work out. Plus, there was no reason I couldn't move her in with me if we really hit it off.

So, we met.

I suspected right off that she'd lied about her age. She looked a good deal older than twenty-six and a good deal older than her online pictures suggested. She had crow's feet, for goodness' sake. Nevertheless, we made our pleasantries and sat down for dinner. Conversation was light. We ordered tea and food and I commented that the place smelled good and she agreed. I asked if she'd written any poetry today and she said the words weren't coming today. When our food arrived, she held up her hand and told me not to start eating yet.

"Bart, I have something to tell you," she said.

I said okay. Surely, she was about to explain that she'd lied about her age, that she'd made her profile say she was twenty-six without realizing what the consequences would be if she really met her true love. She would say the more we talked and the more she realized she was falling in love, the harder it became to come clean. Naturally, this would anger me. But it would be forgivable, I suppose. But I would have to know her real age.

"Bart," she said, looking at her hands, looking at her dinner, looking at her napkin, "I have kids. I have five kids."

I sat dumbfounded, holding a fork with a chunk of slimy red snapper clinging to it, my mouth slightly ajar.

"I'm sorry, Bart. I know I should have told you. But they're really good kids. I think you'll love them."

37

I dropped my fork, took the napkin from my lap and threw it on the table, and got up and left without saying a word, without taking a single bite of dinner. Wendy DarkPoet, or whatever her real name was, called my name and chased me outside. She banged on my window as I pulled out of my parking place. She chased me on foot as I edged out of the lot and shot out onto the freeway.

Unfortunately, Wendy died that night, along with all five of her children and three other residents, when her apartment building burned down. Another artist gone before her time.

A Visitor

40.3% of Uber drivers are female. I did not get one.

It was raining this morning, so I decided to call an Uber to get me to work. I considered driving my mother's old Buick but figured I shouldn't risk it. Sometimes there is a police car parked at the gas station next to Jim's. I'm not sure if the officer is taking a break or watching for violators or randomly looking up license plate numbers to see if the driver of said vehicle has a suspended DL. So, I make the safe decision.

The Uber driver is an African fellow and he

doesn't say a word to me or even nod or otherwise acknowledge my existence when I get in the car. When the door shuts, he drives. We pass Miss Danbury's house and I see her wobbling to the mailbox with an umbrella. She does not slip and fall and break her hip on the wet concrete.

The Uber guy drops me off at Jim's and I tell him thanks for the ride but he doesn't say anything. When I go inside, I'm surprised to find Hector has already arrived. He's dancing around and listening to something on his ear pods as he gets the drive-thru station ready for customers. Jim sees me and asks where I've been. I look at my watch and see that I still have a minute before my shift starts.

Today is Saturday, which means Jim's Hot Chili is 25% off with the purchase of a drink. I get started warming the giant stainless vat we use to cook the chili. Then I go into the cooler and get the plastic tub of chili we've been reheating for at least a week now. It sizzles as I dump it into

Big Bertha, the name we gave the chili-cooking vat. From my pocket I take a zip-lock baggy with a couple of two-day old turds in it and feed it to Big Bertha. The turds sizzle. I stir everything together and place the lid on Big Bertha, then ask Jim if I should make any fresh chili in case we run out. I have raw cat meat in my other pocket just in case. But Jim says the chili should last through the day.

Hector tells me he had two girls at the same time last night, which I'm not sure I believe. I don't question him though. 83% of men want to have a threesome. I'm not one of them. 86% of men lie about their sexual accomplishments. It's probably more. 18% of men claim to have had a threesome. It's probably less.

"Yo, Shorty, that chili smelling good today," Hector says.

I agree, it does. He eats a bowl before our first customer arrives and says it's fantastic. At 11:30, I go to the restroom and take a poop into the same zip-lock baggy then add this to the chili.

Saturdays are busy chili days. Jim has a bowl for lunch. So do Lacy and Rico, the college guy that only works weekends. They all say it's swell. I try a bite for myself and agree it's tasty.

At 5:30pm, thirty minutes until I'm off, Hector comes back to my station and says some girl up front is asking about me. I tell him that's ridiculous and that I'm too busy to play games because I have twelve patties cooking, two of which have cat meat in them. I don't tell him that part.

"Seriously, dog, there's this chick out here asking for you. Has to be you she's talking about."

I sigh and ask him what she said.

"Yo, she said the bald guy with glasses. Yo, she said you found her wallet or some shit."

My mouth drops open. Sweat crops up on my forehead. The sizzle of beef and cat patties seems to grow increasingly loud, until that's all I hear. And I'm hot. It's like it's me on the griddle, being cooked up and flipped and slathered with

cheese and sauce. I haven't a clue what to say.
My mouth likely wouldn't work if I did.

"Yo, it *is* you she's talking about! Shorty, get
your bald ass out there and talk to her!"

I stammer something neither he nor I
understand, standing there slack-jawed with the
spatula in my hand.

"Yo, I'll take over the grill for a minute or
two. Go check her out, Shorty. Get you some of
that poo-nanny!"

Reluctantly, I hand the spatula to Hector
and remove my apron and leave my station in
the kitchen, pushing through the swinging door
that leads to the front registers. The least
desirable profession on the planet when a
woman is looking for a mate is a fast food
worker. That's what I'm thinking as I approach
the counter. It feels odd up here, looking out at
the dining room of Jim's Burger Joint. I never go
to this side of the restaurant.

Sure enough, there she stands. Beaming.

I smile, weakly, my hands clasped in front of

43

my trousers, my fingers fidgeting. It occurs to me that I have a zip-lock bag in my pocket with poop smears inside of it. I hope she can't smell it.

"Hi," she says. Her hands are clasped in front of her too, clutching her purse. "I figured you worked here." She points at her own shirt as if pointing at mine, at the Jim's logo.

I nod but can't manage to say anything.

"I...I wanted to thank you for last night. For giving me my wallet."

I nod again and manage to tell her it was nothing.

"It was very kind of you," she says.

She told me this twice last night and I'm beginning to feel uncomfortable and two customers—two teenagers in slouchy britches—have walked through the door. If they try to place an order with me, I'll look like a complete fool. As they approach the counter, looking at the menu, I point at Jim, who has been standing over in the corner with his arms crossed watching this whole ordeal with amusement, and tell the teens that he'll take their order. Jim chuckles and approaches the register and asks them what they want. I smile again at the woman but feel like I'm smiling too broadly. So, I decrease the broadness of my smile.

"My name is Sara," the woman says.

I nod. She probably thinks I have some mental handicap. I inform her I'm Bart. Then I tell her my whole name is Bartholomew Bartley, just to get that embarrassment out of the way.

"Bartholomew Bartley. What an interesting name. You must have interesting parents."

I agree they were interesting. I don't tell her that Mother died of poisoning and Father died by jumping in front of a bus.

"Bart," she says, looking down at her feet briefly, "would you like to have coffee sometime?"

I stutter something and sound like a fool, like a dark poet. Sara seems to understand whatever garbled mush comes out of my mouth.

"Would tomorrow be okay? Or do you work

45

Sundays? Or go to church?"

I manage to tell her I don't have work and don't go to church. I was forcibly removed from a church once, after an incident involving a rolled-up newspaper, three candles, a priest, and a confessional. But, obviously, I don't tell Sara this.

"Tomorrow then? Starbucks or Carlson's?"

I tell her I prefer Carlson's to Starbucks but we can go to whichever she wants. She prefers Carlson's too. We agree 10am is a suitable time to meet and Sara bids me farewell after once more thanking me for giving her her wallet. Jim says Hell must have frozen over if women are suddenly asking me out on dates. Hector calls me a sly dog and tells me I better be balls deep in Sara by noon tomorrow and tells me I better bring protection if I don't want a little Shorty Jr. crawling around in nine months.

Only 7% of women prefer to ask out the man, as opposed to being asked out.

I float through the rest of my shift. To

celebrate, I treat myself to a chili burger, even though I rarely eat at work. I walk home in a daze. Though Sara didn't say it was a date, that's clearly what it is. You don't ask a stranger to coffee this day and age unless you're considering becoming romantically involved.

Relationships that begin with dates at coffee shops are 71% more likely to be successful than those that begin with dates at pubs. It's a good sign, whether Sara is aware of this statistic or not.

There are no cats in the yard when I arrive home, barely recalling my walk from Jim's to the house. I go through my closet, trying to decide what clothes to wear tomorrow, while listening to a podcast called *The Art of Relationships*. 70% of heterosexual women prefer men who wear clothing that is snug but not tight. Definitely not baggy, unless the woman in question has greater than nine tattoos, two or more piercings in her face, and smokes grass. I should dress casual but not overly casual.

I decide on a pair of dark Levi's and a black button-up shirt that is the proper length to be left untucked. I iron these items while listening to the remainder of the podcast and then hang them up on the back of my bedroom door. Then I polish a pair of black leather shoes that I haven't worn in some time. They're square-toed and fashionable but not too snobbish. After this, I place a black belt and black socks atop my dresser. All of this could have easily been completed tomorrow morning, but I prefer to not be stressed about time.

After a long shower, I pee into a coffee mug and put it in the microwave for eighty-two seconds and put a sleepy time teabag into it. I drink this while watching a documentary about the prevalence of necrophilia in the concentration camps of World War II.

Before going to bed, I send an email to my senator telling him he'll be assassinated in thirteen days. I have trouble getting to sleep, so I stick my finger in my butt and count to fifty.

Date Day

66% of dates in which one of the people in question arrives late result in no follow-up date.

My alarm goes off at 7am rather than the typical 8. After performing my necessaries, I eat a bowl of oatmeal with sliced carrots and mustard, washing it down with apple juice. I wash my mouth twice and shave extra close, being sure not to miss a spot, and apply an extra layer of deodorant. I then dust a small amount of baby powder over my torso and between my legs.

80% of women will not date a man who

stinks. Though, women equally assert they like the scent of a man's sweat, as I stated before. Studies show, however, that the pleasurable sweat odor is noted when a man has been exercising or performing manual labor, not when perspiring from nervousness about a date.

I sit on the couch in my underwear and watch several videos of various surgeries. One of them depicts a large abscess being removed from a man's testicles. When it's 9am, I get dressed and spray on a hint of cologne and once more rinse my mouth with mouthwash.

Given the stats on women's likelihood to date a man without a vehicle, I decide it's worth the risk to take the Buick. Carlson's Coffee is too far to walk and taking an Uber to a date would be ridiculous, and either of those scenarios would be frowned upon by Sara, no doubt. I'll drive the speed limit and stop fully at all stop signs and obey all traffic lights.

I slide into the car and insert the key and for one panicked second I'm convinced the car won't start and my coffee date will be ruined and I'll spend the next three months mourning that I'd lost *the* one, all because I didn't check the Buick's drivability beforehand. But it fires right up.

I worked at a coffee shop for about a year. It was the job I had before my current one. Calling myself a barista sounded a lot better than calling myself a fry cook or burger flipper. 65% of women drink coffee daily. 77% like the smell of coffee. Good numbers. Women—and people in general—hold baristas in higher regard than fast food workers, even though they're both low-paying positions in the food service industry. That job went away when the Texas Department of State Health Services shut down the coffee shop because large volumes of June bugs were being ground up with the coffee beans. It was good coffee.

As I pull up to Carlson's, I see Sara's Honda Accord turning into the parking lot. The fact that she drives a four-door sedan is a good sign, unless there are car seats in back. Women who drive coupes are twice as likely to smoke and drink, and three times as likely to be unfaithful to their mate, compared to women who drive sedans. Women driving minivans are the most loyal, but that's typically a clear indicator of motherhood. I'm not interested in finding a partner who is already a mother.

I park next to Sara and she sees me and waves, smiling, as I put the car in park. We disembark our vehicles at the same time. Sara is wearing a yellow sundress and has a yellow scrunchie holding her hair back. She's wearing makeup, but not much. She wears black flat sandals and her toenails are painted yellow with black polka dots. Her black purse is slung over her shoulder. I tell her good morning.

"Good morning to you, Bart," she says.

We don't touch each other but we walk close together. I feel somewhat awkward, like my hands should be doing something, and I start to put them in my pockets but decide against it, feeling this might give the impression that I don't wish to hold Sara's hand. I ask her how often she goes to Carlson's.

"Not very often," she says, turning her head to look at me as we approach the door. "I usually brew my own. What about you?"

I tell her it's been a while since I've been here and I open the door and allow her to go in first. The coffee shop smells like a coffee shop. Like fresh coffee beans and cinnamon and all manner of sweet things. I tell Sara it smells good.

"Sure does. Have you eaten breakfast? I may get a muffin or something."

I say I ate a little something earlier but that I'm always open to a second breakfast, then I pat both hands on my belly. Sara laughs, smiling broadly. Women find men more attractive when they're capable of poking fun at themselves, especially regarding weight.

We walk up to the counter. Surprisingly, there is no line. I recognize the barista as a young woman whose miniature schnauzer I killed last year. She was reading a book at the city park, letting the pup run about. I cornered it behind some bushes and removed all four of its legs with a pair of garden loppers. It was alive when I left but the newspaper reported the next day that it had died. I still have the legs. Sara orders a vanilla latte and a blueberry muffin. I order a red eye and a brownie. I pay for both orders even though Sara says she is happy to pay.

63% of women prefer the man pay for the meal when on a date, though this stat is trending down.

We take our food and find a table by the window and wait for our coffees. I comment that the weather is nice. Sara says she's glad it stopped raining but that her garden really needed it. I ask what she grows in her garden and she names off several vegetables and some herbs. I tell Sara I had a garden for a few years but that my backyard is in a low area that retains water, so it's not the best for growing. She asks what I grew and I tell her cucumbers. She asks if

54

that's all I grew and I say yes and she laughs and says I must really like cucumbers.

The barista whose dog I killed calls out our order and I go get the coffees. The vanilla latte smells overly sweet. I return to the table and hand Sara the latte and she thanks me and says she likes my glasses. I tell her thank you and tell her her dress is very pretty. We sip at our coffees and nibble at our pastries. We talk about the art that decorates Carlson's, agreeing that it's nice.

"How long have you worked at the burger place?" Sara asks, sounding truly interested.

I tell her almost four years but that I want to become a teacher. I explain that I have most of the college required already and that I just need to enter a teaching program. Sara nods and says that all sounds wonderful. I ask what she does for a living.

"I guess you could say I'm a teacher," Sara says, crinkling her nose in a way that I find alluring. "I make instructional videos."

My heart flutters when she says she's a

teacher. She's getting better by the second. I ask what subjects she covers.

"Oh, all kinds. I'll have to show you. So, do you have any family around here?"

This question is a massive indicator of her intentions. 94% of women who ask about the family of the man they're dating do so because they're interested in a long-term relationship and are curious if current family dynamics could in any way hinder things moving forward. The other 6% ask about family just to fill conversation. I don't believe this is the case.

I tell Sara that I have no children and both my parents are deceased. I tell her about my brother dying when he was an infant, when I was twelve. The official cause of death was SIDS. I don't tell her the real cause. I tell her about my grandfather dying in the nursing home from hypoglycemia. I don't tell her about the large vial of insulin I have in my medicine cabinet. I tell her I have an aunt and uncle that live somewhere in South Dakota who I haven't seen or talked to in years. I ask about her family.

"No kids for me either. Maybe someday. My parents live in Dallas, just far enough away so I can visit on occasion without worrying that they'll drop by without warning."

I laugh at this and we talk some more, sipping our coffees slowly so as not to bring the date to a close too soon. I tell her I collected baseball cards as a kid. She collected rocks and sea shells. I enjoy watching documentaries. She enjoys scary movies and romantic comedies. I have no pets and nor does she, though she likes all manner of animals and would like a pet at some point. I tell her I feel the same way.

I excuse myself to the restroom where I take a leak then stuff a wad of toilet paper down the front of my pants. I look at the fake bulge in the mirror as I wash my hands. When I exit the restroom Sara is looking at her cellphone. Our pastries are long gone and when Sara takes a drink from her mug, I can tell by the tilt angle that it's almost gone.

"Can I have your phone number?" she asks when I get back to the table.

I tell her of course and give her my number. Moments later, my phone buzzes. I look and see that I have a message saying *Hi, Bart!* I text back *Hi, Sara!* and save the number as hers.

"This has been really nice," Sara says, sticking her phone in her purse and smiling at me.

I agree that it certainly has been nice. There is no more coffee in my mug or hers. I'm contemplating how to go about asking Sara for a follow-up date when she speaks.

"When is your next day off?"

I tell her tomorrow, further explaining that Sundays and Mondays are my typical days off, but that I'll pick up Sundays on occasion if I'm wanting a little extra spending money.

"Do you have any plans tomorrow?"

I indicate I don't.

"Would you like to come over to my house then? I can make us lunch and maybe we can watch a movie or something."

89% of women who ask for a second date with a man desire a long-term relationship. 72% of women who ask a man to come to their home are open to the possibility of sex.

Post Date Drama

I'm over the moon with joy after leaving Carlson's Coffee when I see the police car in my rearview mirror, its lights twirling. I'm being pulled over.

Frantically, I look at the speedometer. I was not speeding. I stopped fully at the stop sign half a mile back. I have not been driving erratically. Turning on my turn signal, I slowly pull the Buick into the parking lot of an adult toy store that doesn't open for another hour. When I park, the police car pulls up behind me, blocking me in. Watching through the rearview mirror, I see a female officer disembark from the police car, blonde and slender, wearing sunglasses.

Women in law enforcement are 70% more likely to have a domineering, type A personality as opposed to women in other professions. Though female officers are less likely to use force compared to men, they are twice as likely to write a ticket for simple traffic violations. 22% of female officers are lesbians.

Sighing, I roll down my window as she approaches. Is driving with a suspended license an arrestable offense? I'm not sure. Maybe it's up to the officer. I'm not sure the statistics on female officer arrest rates, but this officer being blonde and slim is not a good sign. Whether I'm arrested or not, the Buick will certainly be impounded, leaving me in quite a predicament tomorrow, when I'm supposed to be going to Sara's for lunch. I could make an excuse to Sara, I suppose, telling her that I had to put the car in the shop or something, and I could take an Uber to her place. But this would result in a serious blow to her perception of my manliness. A man should be able to work on his own car.

"Hello there," the officer says when she reaches my window. "License and proof of insurance, please, sir." Her voice is even, just going through the motions.

Opening my glove box, I grab my insurance card, deciding, for now, not to bother with the revolver or the steak knife or the rope or the Dremel tool I have hidden beneath the car manual. Pulling my license from my wallet, I hand her both items and fart loudly.

82% of women who hear a stranger fart try to avoid interaction with this person.

The officer looks at me oddly, then scrutinizes my license and insurance, both of which are in date. Looking back at me, she says, "Where were you headed, Mr. Bartley?"

I explain that I was going home and had just come from Carlson's.

"I see," the officer says, nodding. "I pulled you over because your brake light is out.

Passenger side."

Relief washes over me. Just a light out. No big deal. I thank the officer for letting me know. I tell her that I'll get it fixed right away. I say I'll go directly to AutoZone and fix it now.

"That's a good idea," she says. "Let me just go run your license and you can get on with your day."

My heart stops. I ask if it's really necessary for her to run my license.

"Have to do it for everyone we pull over. It will only take a minute." She turns and begins walking back to her vehicle.

I call out to her, unbuckling myself and opening the door. Trying not to sound panicked, I ask if she wouldn't mind showing me which light it is that's out.

"It's the passenger side brake light," she says, barely halting her stride back to her vehicle, where she'll quickly discover that my license is suspended.

I get out of the car, saying that I never can

63

remember which light on the Buick is the brake light and which is the blinker. I ask again if she could show me.

Sighing, the officer walks around to the rear of the car and points at the brake light on the right side as I walk up and stand alongside her. I nod and say I thought that was it and suggest that maybe the light is just disconnected and that I should be able to check it out by opening the trunk and that if she didn't mind, she could shine her flashlight into that corner so we can have a look. She sighs again but removes her flashlight from her belt and pushes her sunglasses up on her head.

Smiling, I tell her thank you and open the trunk. The officer clicks her light on and bends inside the trunk, angling the beam to the corner. I ask her what she sees as I pick up the crowbar. She's beginning to say something when I bring the iron crashing down on her head. It makes a crunching wet sound on her skull. She's unconscious after one blow, going limp and nearly sliding out of the trunk. I keep her from falling to the pavement though and lift her and shove her all the way inside. After removing the radio and Glock from her belt, I close the trunk and look around. The parking lot is empty but the street has several cars motoring back and forth. If anyone noticed the happenings, I can't tell.

I throw the radio and gun into the front passenger seat of my car then proceed to the police cruiser that's blocking my escape. It's still running and the doors are unlocked, so I get in and pull it into a parking space. I notice a nightstick wedged in between the seat and the center console and I grab this and put the car in park and turn it off, taking the keys and nightstick with me when I go back to the Buick. I wipe sweat from my brow with the sleeve of my shirt as I start the car and head for home.

I'm about halfway there when I hear the officer start rustling around in the trunk. She bangs on something then screams something I don't understand then bangs on something

65

again. I ask her politely to keep it down. I continue driving normally.

Suddenly, gunshots fill the car, incredibly loud and painful to the ears. Four quick shots from the trunk. One of them tears through the headrest on my seat and I feel it whir past my right ear. Another hits the center of the windshield, leaving a hole with a spider web of cracks around it. Apparently, the officer had another gun on her somewhere.

Screaming a curse that I don't typically use, I grab the Glock from the seat next to me and, still driving, fire into the backseat until all the rounds are spent. Fifteen or sixteen total shots, I think. My ears are ringing, so I can't be sure, but I think the movement from the trunk has ceased.

That night, to celebrate a successful date with Sara, I smear my own feces across my naked body then violate the officer's corpse with her nightstick while I watch a documentary on extreme body modification.

Sara's House

I elect to park the Buick in the street in front of Sara's house rather than in her driveway. Though I installed a new brake light prior to leaving the house, I was unable to get the windshield fixed before today's date. Sara might find the bullet hole in the windshield, the three in the dash, and the multiple bullet holes in the backseat peculiar and parking on the street offers the least likelihood of her noticing these anomalies.

Her house is a moderately sized brick home with light pink trim. The grass in the front yard is lush and manicured and the bushes are neatly trimmed and daffodils along the driveway bloom beautifully. Assuming Sara cares for her yard herself, these things indicate she finds comfort in staying home and takes pride in her things, both of which are ideal traits for a mate.

I'm wearing non-pleated khaki pants and a light blue button-up short sleeved shirt, an outfit I determined looked nice but would be comfortable for sitting—possibly cuddling—on the couch as we watch a movie. There is a strong wind today and it whips my clothing as I get out of the car. The weather man said there is a 70% chance of thunderstorms this afternoon.

56% of women say they are more inclined to get close to their partner during stormy weather.

I walk up the driveway carrying a single red rose—a gift that indicates I like her without coming off as desperate or presumptuous—and move along the sidewalk to the front door, where I ring the bell. Sara answers the door after fourteen seconds. She is wearing another sundress, this one a floral print with lots of reds and yellows. The yellow scrunchie is in her hair again and she wears red lipstick.

59% of women find red lipstick to be empowering. An even greater percentage believe men find red lipstick desirable. This is not the case for me, but her choice of this color suggests she wants my desire.

"Hello, Bart," she says, smiling broadly.

I tell her hello and offer her the rose.

"Thank you so much. That's so sweet." She takes the rose and smells it and sighs with satisfaction. She waves her hand indoors and says, "Come on in."

I follow her inside and close the door gently behind me. There are candles lit somewhere in the house and they smell of frankincense, lavender, and eucalyptus, a combination that conveys neither lust nor romance. It's a homely scent. Comforting. The house is dim but not dark and is well-maintained, clean and tidy without being museum-like.

Sara retrieves a vase from a cabinet in the kitchen and puts an inch or two of water in it and then adds the rose, which she smells once more before turning to me. The kitchen, too, is clean. Whatever she intends to make for lunch, she has yet to begin. I suspect she may want to chat for bit—perhaps even engage in our first kiss— before setting about preparing lunch. This is okay by me.

"Would you like some tea?" she says, pulling a kettle from a cabinet next to the stove. "I always drink a little herbal tea in the afternoon."

I say tea would be wonderful. 35% of women drink herbal tea. People who drink herbal tea are generally believed to be more health conscious and more likely to live a long life.

"I hope you're not too hungry yet. I figured we could drink tea and talk for a little bit first."

I indicate this would be just fine by me. As

the water warms, Sara asks what I did last night. I tell her I did some laundry and watched some television and ate some stew. All this is true. I don't tell her about cleaning the trunk or what I did to the officer or what was in the stew. I tell Sara she has a very nice house and she says thank you and says we'll go look at the garden later if I want and I say that would be fine. She says she has some cucumbers in the garden but they're not ready to be picked yet.

When the kettle whistle blows, Sara grabs two mugs and adds a teabag to each and pours in the water. She hands me one and leads the way into the living room where we settle onto the couch, sitting apart but not too far apart. Conversation continues over this and that. I sip at my tea and she sips at hers. I ask what her favorite kind of music is. She says golden oldies, like Van Morrison and The Everly Brothers and John Denver. I state she has good taste in music and she puts some on, keeping it low so we can still talk.

Studies show that people who prefer mellow music are more empathetic and observant of the needs of others.

I yawn but Sara appears not to notice. She tells me about a time when she visited Alaska with her parents, but I'm having trouble following her story. The music, even though it's low, seems to weave in and out of her words. I watch Sara's lips moving, trying to read the words as well as hear them. I yawn again. I'm incredibly embarrassed and apologize for yawning but Sara waves her hand and continues talking. Now, she's telling me about a trip to Hawaii, saying how blue the water was and something else and more stuff I don't follow. My brain is foggy. I try to remember if I got any sleep last night after everything I did with the officer. I can't remember. My eyelids are growing heavy. Sara's words are garbled; mushy sounding.

43% of men report having a drink unknowingly spiked at some point in their life. A shocking statistic.

Perfect Match

I'm naked when I wake up.

There is a bright light above me, shining down on me, like the lights in those surgical shows I watch. My brain is still muddled and my arms and legs aren't moving. I realize I'm restrained. I'm lying on something—a cold slab of metal, it feels like—and my arms are restrained at one end and my legs at the other.

"There he is," I hear Sara say from my right. "I was wondering when you would come around, Bart."

I look in that direction, my vision blurry. I

blink several times, hoping to understand what I'm looking at. Sara is outfitted in black latex. The latex suit even stretches over her head, leaving openings over her mouth, nose, and eyes. Her lips look red as ever. She has some sort of military style hat on her head. She fancies herself a dominatrix, I'm guessing.

16% of women enjoy bondage. I'm unsure if that statistic means enduring the bondage, applying the bondage, or both.

This is an unexpected development.

Though my words are slurred, I manage to ask Sara what's going on.

"Oh, Bart," she says, flinging her hand up. It's then that I realize she's holding something. Some leather thing with tassels. A flogger? "You've been chosen to participate in one of my lessons!"

I should be very concerned about where this is headed—and I am—but for some reason I can't help picturing my naked self laid out like this. I'm thinking about what my penis must look like with me being cold and scared and embarrassed. I'm certain it has sucked itself up into my abdomen somewhere. This is very humiliating. I let Sara know that I appreciate her wanting to involve me in her lesson but that I'm very cold and kind of just want to go home.

She laughs and turns around and looks at something. I realize there is a camera behind her. A camera on a tripod. A green light is on, I guess indicating that it's recording. My vision is clearing a little. At least she left my glasses on. I sigh and look back up at the light, noticing another camera up there. Looking back at Sara, I suggest maybe we could do this another day.

"I think not," she says, laughing again. "Bart, have a look to your left."

I have a look to my left. The wall is covered with things. Leather things and stainless things and other stuff. Whips and paddles and saws and knives and surgical instruments. All manner of things one would expect in a sufficiently stocked torture chamber.

1.2% of women consider themselves sadistic.

I congratulate Sara on her assortment of things and ask if she plans on hurting me.

She laughs again, then turns to the camera. "Ladies and gentlemen, boys and girls, people of every sort, this is a lesson on what happens when you're a naughty boy. Do you want to see what I do to bad little boys? Do you want to learn how *you* should treat bad little boys? Of course you do!"

She twirls her leather thing for the camera then spins around and hits my chest with it. It doesn't hurt bad. She tosses it aside and leaves my field of vision. That was just for show, I'm assuming. I ask Sara what I did to be a bad little boy. I tell her I thought we had a good date. I say I don't think I deserve this.

She emerges again, leaning over my face and whispering, "You didn't do shit, Bart. You're a good little boy. I just say that shit for the camera." With that, she shoves something into my mouth, something plastic and tube-like. She turns back to the camera. "This one comes by special request from Johnny in Iowa: The Funnel of Puke!"

My mind is just beginning to register what she's said when I see Sara's latex-covered fingers diving into her own mouth, gagging her. She gags and leans over me, removing her hand and vomiting directly into the funnel she's stuffed into my mouth. It's hot and sour and chunky, filling my mouth and gagging me. I try to spit it out but Sara has a firm hold on the funnel, making it impossible for me to expel anything. I have only one choice: I swallow the puke. It immediately regurgitates back into my mouth, but with nowhere for it to go, I force it back down. Three times I throw up into my mouth and have to swallow. Eventually, it stays. Sara removes the funnel and tells me that wasn't so bad. Panting, I say it was pretty bad. She says we're just beginning.

It doesn't get better from there. Sara

smashes my balls with a hammer. She saws off my toes. She sticks needles in my eyeballs. Of course, she whips me and paddles me and flogs me and all that stuff too. All of this, apparently, is at the request of different people from different places. Her patrons, I suppose. Or students, she may call them. She pulls out my teeth with pliers and runs screws up my nose and cuts my penis off and shoves it up my butt and uses a giant dildo to shove it up further. Lots of people requested butt stuff. All sorts of things get shoved up there. At one point, Sara pulls poop out of my butt and smears it on me. I find it somewhat ironic that I was enjoying doing that to myself the night before.

I don't last long when the knives come out and she starts exploring my insides. I'm assuming the video lasts a good while after I'm dead. No reason for her to stop just because my heart does.

0.000000006% of women in the United States make a living doing snuff films. And that

one lady just happens to be my perfect match.
My 100% match.

ABOUT THE AUTHOR

Patrick C. Harrison III (PC3) is an author of horror, splatterpunk, and all forms of speculative fiction. He is also an award-winning editor and a blogger. You can follow his free newsletter at pc3horror.substack.com, where he writes frequent movie reviews and updates on his fiction. If you're interested in either his writing or editing services, feel free to email PC3 at pc3@pc3horror.com.

More Books from PC3

Grandpappy
Vampire Nuns Behind Bars
A Savage Breed
Cerberus Rising (w/ Chris Miller & M. Ennenbach)
Inferno Bound and the Hell Hounds
5 Tales That Will Land You in Hell
5 Tales of Tantalizing Terror
Visceral: Collected Flesh (w/ Christine Morgan)
Visceral 2: Filleted Flesh (w/ Daniel J. Volpe)

If you enjoyed *100% Match*, you're guaranteed to be a fan of PC3's exceedingly depraved novella *Grandpappy*. Find it on Amazon!

Praise for *Grandpappy:*

"PC3 unleashes the equivalent of an Extreme Horror nuclear bomb on fans of the genre. The result is a cyclone filled to the dirty brim with brutal imagery and gorrific dialogue, all wrapped in a filthy, overflowed adult diaper worn by the legendary Grandpappy!"
-K. Trap Jones, author of *The Drunken Exorcist* and owner of The Evil Cookie Publishing

"Well. That was f*cked."
-M Ennenbach, a thoroughly disgusted poet and author of *Hunger on the Chisolm Trail*

"With a level of grotesquery matched only by its pitch-black hilarity, Grandpappy manages to

tell a story so interesting you ALMOST forget about all the...moist bits."
-Chris Miller, author of *Dust* and *Shattered Skies*

"I can't in good conscience give *Grandpappy* a blind recommendation to the Gen Pop, but for the weirdos, splatterpunks, and fans of extreme, I think it's requisite reading. It's the twisted bastard child of *The Nightly Disease, House of Leaves*, and *American Psycho* — but much sicker than any of those titles."
-Craig Wade, Host of B-Movies and E-Books

"One of the most extreme, twisted, splattery pieces of fiction to ever come out. This book will have you thanking whatever God you worship, that you don't have a Grandpappy like this to care for. If you have a weak resolve or stomach, consider this your warning."
-Dawn Shea, owner of D&T Publishing

"A stomach-churning good time. PC3 knows

how to cut the gross-outs with a healthy dose of humor. This is the kind of book that'll have you giggling into your barf bag (but keep one handy, yeah?)" -Brian Asman, author of *Man, F*ck This House*

"Patrick C. Harrison III's prose are smooth, engaging, and lull you into a false sense of wholesomeness. *Grandpappy* puts the reader through the emotional ringer, and then squeezes out a little bit extra for good measure. If you're looking for your next read that leaves no stone unturned, and no taboo unexplored, *Grandpappy* is sure to tick all the boxes. From the most unreliable narrator I've ever read, to medical terms that I had to look up and then wished I could scrub from my mind, Harrison takes you places you never thought you'd go. 5 rancid beans out of 5. P.S. As for me, chilidogs are now OFF the menu." -RJ Roles, owner/operator of Books of Horror and Crimson Pinnacle Press

"In *Grandpappy*, PC3 practically pries open your eyelids and force feeds drops of acid into your eyeballs as he whips this wicked written fever dream across the page. It's imaginative, intense, and totally insane. You'll vomit in your mouth a bit, but you'll f*ckin' love it."
-Carver Pike, author of *Grad Night* and co-host of the Written in Red Podcast

"I'm a registered nurse. I've dealt with the colostomies. The dreaded bedsores. The gnarly fungus-encrusted toenails. And yes...the smells. Inexplicably, PC3 still managed to stimulate my gag reflex throughout the entirety of this story. Bastard."
-Bridgett Nelson, author of *Bouquet of Viscera*

"Crazy! Out of this world weird at times. It goes from a normal start to suspicion of the weird, to what just happened!?
This book is not for everyone, it is truly

extreme. If you dare, you may be rewarded. Or
you may be sick. Either way it will be an
unforgettable experience."
-Amazon Review

"I loved this book!! It was like a splatterpunk
fever dream. It was my first by the author but
won't be my last. If you like absurd and gross
horror this book is for you."
-Amazon Review

"What the hell was that? Wild ass book, that
read more like a Bizzaro Extreme Horror.
Messed with my head a LOT. That being said, it
was a fun read, and made ME feel like I was
going crazy."
-Goodreads Review

Made in the USA
Middletown, DE
08 September 2024

60419353R00060